You were a Reason

A Love Story in Prose

Heather Bigoraj

DEDICATION

Dedicated to my sister Tammy

Who said
"I believe you can do anything you want. Always"

My eternal cheerleader

ACKNOWLEDGMENTS

Thank you to my friend (Taralee) for the support. From the start of this journey, you were there with guidance helping me create this book.

To my sister (Tammy), niece (Shelby) and the other supportive friends who read the final draft and gave amazing feedback, thank you, you made the feeling of capturing an audience's attention real.

This accomplishment would not have been possible without each one of you. Your encouragement, love, and belief in me have been my motivation, and for that, I am forever grateful.

PRELUDE

"What's it like when you fall in love?"
She asked the wind, blowing in the trees
"What's it like when you feel safe in love?"
She asked the skies of the brightest blue

Does your heart feel happy and does your loneliness stop?

"Yes child, it feels timeless,
Like a calm that fills your heart"
The Universe whispered back to her, ever so quietly
Through the rustling of leaves

"I hope to feel that kind of love one day" she replied.

She heard the quietest whisper back
"Here, let me show you"

Were you my Lifetime
Or just a Reason?
-

The stars in the sky
Twinkling with secrets
Along with
the Universe
Full of all space and time
Knew the answer
-

My fate was sealed

YOU WERE A REASON

PART 1

YOU WERE A REASON

Falling in love is the easiest thing to do,
When your heart has found its home.
-

H. Bigoraj

It was you
Your face in a photo
My heart beat fast
That feeling of familiarity

A rush of jealousy
At the woman cuddled up to you
How did she have your heart
When I knew it should be mine

Your eyes
The color of blueberries
Sparkling with happiness
I wanted to make you happy like that

Your tattoos silently speaking words to me
The bird on your neck
Like a sign from the Universe

Reminded me of the psychic who said
"Listen to the birds as they sing, they are trying to tell you something"

Did they know
That you would have my heart one day?

So familiar
Like I had known you before
In another life
In another time
Our souls fused together from another place

A chance meeting coming years later
The stars lined up
The Universe playing matchmaker

Swiping left or right
I see you
My heart speeds up

My mind races
As I think back to your happiness in those photos
I wonder why you were there

Smiling as I swiped right
An instant response
A match

The messaging never slowed
Quick to ask me on a date
Excited to meet me

"I will plan it all" you said
"It will be a night you will never forget"

I felt an ease in saying yes to you planning
Something so masculine and confident
Strong and sexy

The first date
The best I've ever had

The fireworks on a warm summer's night
Country music playing in the background
The river flowing to the left of us

The stars twinkling in the darkness
A full moon shining in the distance
We danced and kissed in the park
Your hands running up and down my back

A romantic's paradise

As we swayed to the music
Your words whispered in my ear
Words so wicked they started a fire
Tangled in my memory for eternity

My mind questioning
How could this date be so simple yet so perfect

The night lasted forever
And at the same time was over in a second

I've never felt a color from someone
You were purple
You tasted like lavender

Was that your aura?
It was intoxicating

Your energy powerful
Yet soft

Knowing in that moment
The Universe put us together
-

Kismet

"Come away with me" you asked
"Imagine that as a second date"
Your eyes bright from the moonlight
Searching mine for an answer
Full of hope and need

Saying yes meant the start of something
Between us
Saying no meant saying goodbye to you
-
It was the easiest yes ever spoken

To this day
The smell of my perfume takes me back
On a wave of memories

To our second date

To a time in the sun on a boat
A magical place
Kokomo playing on the radio
As we loved each other in the summer heat

We skipped rocks on the lake
While having morning coffee
The excitement you had from skipping a seven

We lazed on the beaches
The water warmed by the sun
Giving us an escape
From the summer fever

Holding hands on walks
Your eagerness to show me all the sights and spots
Of the paradise you found
Wanting to share it with me

Surrounded by mountains
The smell of cedar
Evening thunderstorms
Bringing out the smells of the forest

This was paradise

Nights so hot we wore as little as possible
Laying on the dock and holding hands
Dipping our feet in the water
Letting them be kissed by the waves

Watching the stars twinkle
Calling out the constellations
Creating names for ones we didn't know
Our laughter echoing through the night

An owl sitting in the cedars
Hoots
The loons on the lake
A beautiful song

Lightning bugs
Floating through the darkness
Adding a twinkle of magic

Rolling on your side to me
You kiss me
Slow and full of heart

Into the early morning
Watching the sunrise
Over the mountains
Bringing sparkles to life

The promise of a new day
New adventures
Precious time to learn who we were to each other

So carefree
So new
The sweetness of your excitement
Adding butterflies to my heart
-
I could have stayed frozen in that time

You said you had never felt this before
That I was someone special
How could I be so perfect?
-
So easy to believe when you are in paradise
The real world a thousand miles away

Seven days in paradise
With you
My skin sunkissed and my heart full

At the airport, leaving felt wrong
I cried
Scared of what leaving meant
The possibility of the end

Brushing away my tears with your thumbs
Hugging and swaying to our own music
You whisper "I had so much fun with you"
My mind racing, expecting the next words to be goodbye
Forever

Your next words
Like a lightning bolt to the heart
You spoke

"I am all yours, if you want me"

Oh, how I wanted
I had never wanted something so much in my life

Time seemed to speed
Seasons changed faster
I wanted it to slow down

To savor the love growing
And yet, I wanted to run
As fast as I could

Into your arms
Into your love
For the rest of my life
-
You felt like home

Christmas came
More days spent in heaven
Seeing the sights of the city
Skating in the outdoor park
As the trees twinkled with lights
Putting the childlike excitement of Christmas back in my heart

We watched old movies
Your favorites as a child
Your house over dressed in Christmas
Showing a side of you I had not seen
A softness I wanted to be wrapped in

A night at a hotel
Champagne glasses clinking
The lights off
Watching the city roar below from the penthouse suite
The scene out of a movie

The season holding new promises
Of what could be
Promises of a future for us

My heart filling with love
Hoping you would say those words to me
They didn't come from your lips
I felt it though

The New Years eve party I didn't want to attend
Nervous to meet your friends
You would never leave my side you promised
That look you gave me
Of words unsaid

You casually greet the host
Introducing me as your girlfriend
My mind froze
Stuck on those words
Hearing them for the first time
My heart explodes with happiness

The rest of the night
While we mingled
Your eyes kept finding mine

I was yours
Branded
By the need in your eyes

Under the mistletoe
Your lips brushing mine
Created fire in my veins

Every muscle in your body pinned against mine
Your hands on my hips, pulling me closer to you
I grabbed on never wanting to let go

Your cologne
I smelled in my hair the next day
When I catch a scent of that cologne
-

It reminds me of you

We left that party early

Every stoplight you lean in to kiss me
Your hand cups my chin

Whispering wicked words against my mouth
Things you wanted to do
When we got "home"

The anticipation
Growing in my stomach

Making love till the birds started singing
You asked if I thought the birds talked
Their beautiful melodies surely meant something

I was reminded of the man

What were the birds saying to us
Were they telling us we were meant to be
That the right love had finally found me
-

And it was you?

Because
You felt like forever
Felt like calm
Felt like a thousand unspoken words
That I needed to hear

In the morning light
You said the three words
Kissing my forehead
Resting your head on my chest in vulnerability

With those three words
I knew my life would never be the same

We slept in
Waking up next to you
Feeling safe
The comfort I had never felt before

You woke and pulled me closer
Snuggling into you
Tracing the outline of the tattoos on your arm
One of my favorite past times

"I promise I won't ever hurt you"
You whispered to me
Through kisses on my shoulder

Those words went through to my soul
I believed them
-
How could I not?

YOU WERE A REASON

New Years Day
You wanted to celebrate
365 new days to spend with me
I happily accepted

As I slid lipstick over my lips
Thinking of your kisses and the words spoken from your mouth
Biting my lower lip with anticipation
Knowing more were coming

You bought flowers
Your kindness was heartwarming
I floated the rest of the night

How you made me feel important
So effortlessly
How you made me feel seen
So freeing

Your words at dinner still play as music in my memory
That my touch was fire yet calming
I was all you would ever need
How you dreamed of a woman like me

"Please don't hurt my heart" you whispered in my ear
In that moment I felt the need to protect you
I vowed never to hurt you
How could I
To be so open and soft
Your vulnerability something new and foreign to me

This man that I loved
Who told me he loved me
How could I ever hurt you?

A master with your words
I fell hard and fast
I didn't try to fight it
I wished for the wind to push me faster
Into eternity with you

That is when

I fell….

Like a feather

Floating

Falling

Into the Abyss

Of your love

I brought the last wall down
You had my whole heart

I would gladly give you my soul
Trusting you with everything that I was

You consumed me
And I wanted to feel this

Forever

I was
Drunk on your love

You

Showed me how a man could have emotions
And speak of them with words
Speak with conviction but use kindness
Have calm but confident energy

You anticipated needs
Made plans
Put thought into my happiness
Date nights and day dates

You made me feel protected
And most important
Safe
Such simple things
That held more meaning than you will ever know

I never trusted someone
To love me how I deserved
None had shown they could until

You

How could I put into words
Something I never felt before

How could I tell you
Something so vulnerable

That no man had
loved me the way you did

And more important
-
No man before you deserved my love

Explaining you to friends
How perfect you were
Every sweet thing you did
To show you cared

They said it was the bare minimum
That I should expect more

Why weren't those enough?

The feeling of happiness
Of being wanted
Of being loved
Being seen was the ceiling in my world

What else was I to expect
What was higher than that bar
You were the highest bar I had known

I chose to ignore them
They didn't understand you
Your love
-
They were wrong, right?

Toying with this dose of reality
I chose to ignore
The fulfillment of you
Was louder than their words

The heat from the summer sun back
We walk downtown
Outdoor patios on
Cobblestone streets

A man plays guitar on the corner
The crowds walk by
Tossing coins into his guitar case
Hidden by a big umbrella
We people watch, making life stories of strangers

Our cheeks sore
Laughing in the summer light
Holding my hand at the table
You lean over and kiss me

You lean back and look at me
The look of love and something else
I can't quite put a word to

"I love you I want you to know that"

I laugh and reply
"I know that silly"
Playfully pushing your shoulder
I kiss your cheek

The tone you used
Different than before
Gave me pause
I tell myself I'm overthinking
That your love is growing for me

Late in the summer
The air starting to cool
The days getting shorter
A weekend getaway

It was raining
You with your red umbrella
Walk me to the car
Opening the door
Kissing the tip of my nose

Ever the gentleman

The weather changing with our excitement of the weekend
Like it could sense the eagerness
The new love
Wanting to enjoy the days with us
The clouds moving away

The drive to the mountains full of laughter

The question I never tired of asking
"Where have you been all my life"
You look over at me and smile that beautiful smile
You grab my hand and kiss it
And answer the same every time

"On my way to you babe"

I still hear your voice
Saying those words
Deep and raspy
Sexy

In the sun filled afternoon
Snow capped mountains all around us
Leaves turning colors of golds, reds and browns
From the cold crisp night air

We boated to an island
You laid out a blanket
Your perfectly planned day date

Music playing
Watching the waves slowly lap the shoreline

Once again, in paradise

Wine and food made us hazy
We made love on that island

Laying with my head on your shoulder
Tracing the lines of my favorite spot on you
The dip between the muscles on your chest

Stopping my hand on your heart
"You make my heart happy
Can you feel how happy it is?" you asked

Ever the romantic

How did you know what to do in every moment
What to say to make my heart beat fast
To make me feel like the most special woman on earth

The cabin
Smelling of wood
The fireplace
Holding promises of a perfect night

You cook while we drink wine
Music playing
Fire crackling
We slow danced in the kitchen

The table for two
An exquisite supper
In our own little world
Tucked away for the night

Pillows by the fire
Laying in your arms
Slowly tracing your muscles
"Your touch is so calming" you whisper

Your slow heartfelt kisses
Bringing tears to my eyes
I felt so much love from you
I could never feel this way with another
-
I tell myself

The early morning hours
Sneak up on us
One minute the sun sets
The next minute it rises

How does time move so fast with you?

We talked through night
Telling stories of our past
Childhood memories

Hopes and dreams
How we see the future
Together, forever? I ask

Nervous of your reaction
I gaze your way
Your blueberry eyes
Flickering with flames from the fire
Looking at me
Really seeing me

You laugh
Kissing my forehead
"It's crossed my mind too"
-
Never surer, He is my lifetime

I would travel to any end of the earth
To find you
The way you made me feel
I would chase it for an eternity

Telling you that
You smile
Your eyes light up
Holding all our secrets

You tell me you love me

I promise myself
To my dying day
Nothing will sound better than your voice
Saying those three words

In our chapter, I lost myself

And I was fine with losing myself
She was addicted to the feeling you gave her

The feeling She never felt before
The feeling of acceptance
Of being seen
Those feelings better than "Love"

You were my undoing

I would have given you everything
I tried to give you everything

But in the end
Maybe my love wasn't enough

PART 2

"I wish I had met you before you were broken
You hid it so well"

-

H. Bigoraj

With the fall
A season of cooling
A season of change
I felt it
-
Your heart becoming distant

The love affair was closing
I felt you pulling away
In the lapse of phone call
The text messages shorter
The response time in between becoming longer

Remembering details about my life
Asking about my day or upcoming plans
Gone

The reasons of being so busy
Or too tired to talk
What's more hurtful than being cut from someone's life
Are the polite and easy lies that are given

I found solace in the maybes
Pleading with myself to believe your reasons
It hurt less if I believed your half-hearted responses

I couldn't lose you
Overwhelmed with the fear of what life would be with out you
Panic set in
I tried to give you space
If I did, you would miss me, right?

It didn't work

In the end
Your heart was already closed
-
To me

Too scared to confront your actions

-

Too scared to lose you
I let you control the ending

-

I wish I fought to choose the ending

It was over

I didn't want to admit that
Because if it was over then everything we experienced was flawed
And that meant you were flawed
Something I had never seen in you before

But your flaws were held behind your facade

My heart pierced with the ice you used to end it
How cold you were
In a text message
Abrupt

The answer to the question
"Why"
Never given
My mind created reasons
To satisfy the pain
But no reason ever really sufficed

How you were able to turn yourself into a stranger
Almost overnight
Leaving no room to challenge your decision
The door closed

Confused by the two sides of you
Scrutinizing our love
Became a favorite pastime

The Men you were
The one I thought I knew
And the one you hid

I can't reconcile the two into one man

You were the good guy
The lover
The protector

You were also a fraud
You were broken
You tried to love
A failed experiment on me

Was it me
Was it love
What scared you away?

I deserved answers
But in the end, any answer given
Wouldn't have satisfied
The pain you left
-
Was it all a lie?

How do you let go
Of something
That made you feel whole
That made you complete

How do you erase memories
That felt like home
And at the same time
Brought pain

Easy to stay stuck in the familiar
There is comfort there

Broken and Burned
Curled on the floor
Gasping for air
From the heaving sobs

Would the pain ever stop?
I wasn't prepared to lose you
I felt blindsided

The broken pieces of my heart
Leaking through my tears
Escaping me
Uncontrollable

Why would fate bring us together
Then cruelly tear us apart
-
An answer I needed from the Universe

I tried to leave you on the beaches of Galveston
Saying goodbye as the waves crashed into the rocks
It seemed like the perfect place
Leave paradise in paradise

Where the sky meets the ocean
Using conviction and all the strength I could muster
I tried not cry, my voice full of pain
I speak for the first time since we sat
Telling my friend that I was leaving you on the pier

I was ready to release the memories
Where the sun shone
Where the saltwater
Carried by the wind
Sprayed up and around me

Like a rebirth
It was a new beginning

As much as it hurt
I was determined to leave your memory in the space of the unknown
Where the sea could wash away the pain
Of perfect memories
-
And what could have been

The sea didn't wash you away
I let your memory follow me
To the crowds in New Orleans

Trying to share my experience with you
To get you to engage
Your response to my pictures was lifeless
Causal like a stranger

Watching the parades move down the most famous streets in the world
All the purples and greens
The colors of Mardi Gras
The purple reminding me of our first kisses
Your taste
Like lavender

My heart broke again
The thumping of the drums keeping beat with my exploding heart
Trying to hold back the tears
The sunglasses blocking what I needed to hide

For too long
I tried to find a way back into your life
My heart kept trying to find the man I first met
Find a semblance of you

For too long
I tried to find you
I searched in the crowds
In everything I experienced
In the beautiful places visited

I listened for your voice
I breathed in the scents
Hoping I would smell you
Again

I looked for you
I prayed for you
To magically appear
-
And take my heartache away

Sitting in a coffee shop
Staring out into the street
I see a man and woman walking in the rain
He holds the red umbrella

A memory comes to mind
My heart stops

I cry

Friends convince me to meet someone new
I go on a date
Cobblestone streets and a patio view
I try to focus on the present

More memories flood
My heart breaks again

I cry

You text one rainy day
My heart stopped when I seen your name
A simple
"Hey"

Fingers trembling, I text back
Asking what you need

An attempt to apologize
"Sorry, I never meant to hurt you"
The sentence blurring through my tears
The words meaningless

But my heart sees a glimmer of hope

I want you to admit you made a mistake
That you missed me
Life was empty without me
I was your Forever

Your intention different from my hope
Your apology meaningless
Confusing

My heart shattered anew
Tears flowed
Any progress made
Destroyed by seven simple words

As fast as you left the first time
You disappeared again, for the final time
Allowing no opening for me
To say how I felt

Would it have mattered
To know how destroyed I was
By you

I yearned to know
How long you planned
To break my heart and to shatter a love
-
That was meant to last a lifetime

For a Season
I had felt sorry for you
Knowing how you became broken
The story raw within your words

Your soft heart
Wearing your last heartbreak

You sat in your pain
It was comfortable punishment
Believing you deserved it

Using it as a shield
Your ultimate excuse
Unsure if you could love again

I wanted to shelter your heart
Help you heal
Protect you
But I should have protected myself

I tried to show you I was different
I would never hurt you like your last love
But you never believed
-
You weren't ready to

The pain subsides
Anger follows
For lying
For leaving
-

For breaking my heart

I could blame you
For taking the part of me
Who was full of peace and happiness
But I gave it freely
Because it was you
The man who wished on the same stars
Who came to me in my dreams
-

Who felt like home

I gave myself to you
For a chance at a feeling
-

Love

And for those reasons
I could not hate you
and
I could not erase
The memories of
you

I wonder if your heart hurt
If you missed me

Do you search for a love like mine
Something so pure
Soulful

Do you miss the woman
Who had you on a pedestal
Who thought you were the world
Who would have loved you eternally

Do you stare up at the night sky
Hoping I was wishing on the same star
Do you ask the Universe to bring us together again
-
Asking for a second chance?

I wonder if
One day, years later
We met by accident

On the same cobblestone streets
Where we fell in love
Our heartbeats matching again

Would looking at you still feel like Home
Would we see an unspoken lifetime in each others' eyes?

Would we part ways and think
What if

What if we had tried to save it
What if our love would have been enough for you?

I fear I would smell your cologne
And the love would come back
I fear we would hug
And I would feel your strength

Lost in a thousand what ifs
We would part ways
-
Lovers once but strangers now

Revelations are the Universe at work

And, after time
I realized
What I thought was a Lifetime
Was only a Reason

You were not meant to stay

You gave me the gift
To see
How beautiful love can be

The dream of growing old together
Living our days in love
Watching you grow old next to me
Gone

The what if you were my Lifetime
Answered

And after a long Season
-
I was at peace with that answer

PART 3

"Acceptance
An unexpected gift after a broken heart"
-

H. Bigoraj

Convincing myself I was healed
I tried to move on

Another man's words against my ear
I want to cry out your name

His hands on my body
Leave me feeling empty

They weren't the hands
That once filled me with Love

Attempting intimacy
When the heart isn't healed
Devastating
-
I wondered if I ever would be

The clouds turn dark
Raindrops on the window
I feel empty
Lost

Scared of the unknown
I reach out to unconditional love
My sister

My safe space
To speak
My darkest feelings
Without judgment

The fear to end up
Unloved
Alone

"What if I'm broken
What if I never feel love like that again?"

"You will, because you are trying"
Was her answer
"And, more importantly, you deserve it"

With that answer
A sliver of light shines
Through the slices of my broken heart
Like the Three of Swords in a tarot deck

Reminding me
We survive storms that teach lessons
Heartbreak fades
New possibilities emerge
-
The Heart will always heal

I used to crave Fall
The cold air changing the landscape
Taking me back to memories made
Of a love so tender and sweet

To sit in the memories
Sit in my heartbreak
Such a familiar place
Was comfort at times

The pain of
repeating memories
The feelings
The words
The touches
-
A beautiful torture

But what if
After time
The place that was once comfort
Became vacant
It felt foreign

Hollow
Somehow it was no longer me
A place that was once my home
No longer existed

The hit I got from the memories of you
Stopped giving me the same high
-
The drug of you stopped working

Slowly, the changing of the seasons
Begin to feel like
The changing of chapters

The colors
The smells
The air

After a season of darkness
Like a dark tumultuous sky
That matched my shattered heart
The clouds eventually leave

The sunlight seems brighter
The sky blue again
The clouds light and puffy

The birds
Singing their melodies
Swooping past me
Getting my attention

I wonder
With anticipation
What they want to tell me

The Universe showing
Opportunities of a new chapter
Planned for me
Synchronicities and coincidences

The humming of energy
Feeling the vibrations
Rumble through my body
Pushing me forward

Butterflies in my stomach
Excitement for the future
I smile
-

I learned the secret

A new Season here
I watch the rain soak the earth
A glass of wine
Scents from a candle enveloping me

I smile, knowing
I found my peace and happiness again

Gratefulness seeps through me
All that I have learned
How I have healed
Since a flawed love

Experiences gained
Goals made and achieved
Friends empowering me

Spiritually aware
Accepting of the Universe
That it removes what doesn't belong
To open the doors for better
-

I know I am healed

For a period
Time wasted brought regret
-

But the Season that passed
I had to travel through

To become a stronger Me
-

Time wasted becomes
Treasured experience

The lost woman, replaced
This new woman I see

Is someone stronger
Who knows
What she needs in love

It's Effort

Knowing it's Me

Choosing Me

Every day

AFTERWARD

The Invisible String Theory
Idyllic
Soulmates moving through life
Toward each other

And one day
It happens
The connection

The hopeless romantic I am
Evaluating every man
Was he the one, my fairytale prince?
The one who questions "where has she been all my life"?

But the potential princes
Turn into toads
Time unveiling their warts
Shining brightly like a badge of honor

After the toads and the tears
I decided to let go
Allow Love to reveal itself

Maybe
I was running and Love was walking
I needed to adjust my pace to meet it
-
Let the Universe take the lead

One night, wishing upon the stars in the sky
The full moon that once brought me so much love
Was shining brightly
My prayers flowing up with the wind up to the twinkling lights above
Riding on the streaks of shooting stars

That night, my wish felt different
It felt answered
What if our souls were wishing upon the same stars that night
Wishing our next life choices would bring us to each other

I opened my heart to the flow

The Universe, in its beautiful, infinite wisdom
Shows signs when you are on the right path
Trying to share Its secrets

And, if you are listening and the stars align….

The Love, oh the Love we get to share
The most beautiful thing on earth

It's a Love I would live over and over again

And one day
There he was
My Lifetime

Who highlighted the light in the sky
Making the world bright
Morning sunrises with so much sparkle on the grass and trees
That my eyes blurred

A new Love so happy and beautiful
That I wonder why
Why I thought the Love I experienced before
Was the ceiling

Waiting in line for my coffee
To pass the time
I gaze in the crowd to look at the strangers
I see his face

The black uniform and badge
Adding a sex appeal to the confident aura
The light hazel of his eyes
Growing dark when we caught gazes

Walking to stand by me
He breaks the silence
"Come here often?" he asked
A terrible joke

Ever the charmer

I laugh, a little too loud
His eyes light up in surprise
A smile catches up
The look we share
Makes me pause

What if
-
He was part of the plan all along

With my coffee I find a seat
Stopping at my table on his way out
With a note
His number

"I hope you'll use this"
And with a wink he was gone
Smiling
I open my phone

An immediate response from him
That said

"This is a good "how we first met" story
I have a feeling the next chapter
Is going to be a great one"

And when he said
"I loved you since the moment we met"
I knew for certain

The Universe conspired
With the dreams and wishes
With the frogs and the Princes
-
The Invisible String Theory was revealed.

Standing on the mountain ridge
Watching the birds
Hundreds of feet below
Dip into the aqua blue pond
She heard the faint whispering of the wind

"You found it."

"What if it's taken away from me?" she asked
The unending sky meeting the mountain peaks

"It won't be, It was meant for you"

"What do we do now?" she asked

"Enjoy the secret, sweet child" whispered the Universe

.Enjoy the Love.

ABOUT THE AUTHOR

Heather is a writer based in Calgary, Alberta. There she draws inspiration from the Canadian Rockies and the vibrant culture of the city. With a passion for storytelling and prose, she captivates readers with whimsical and compelling poetry.
When she's not writing, she enjoys spending time outdoors, hiking and travelling.

Manufactured by Amazon.ca
Acheson, AB

16187039R00060